I Play

Colin Dowland
Illustrated by Jess Mikhail

On Monday, I play ping-pong with a bat.

But I do not win!

On Tuesday, I play snap with a crab.

But I do not win!

On Wednesday, I play chess with a king.

But I do not win!

On Thursday, I play dot-to-dot with a pen.

But I do not win!

On Friday, I play tag
with a dog.

But I do not win!

On Saturday, I play up with my dad.

But I do not win!

On Sunday, I play hide-and-seek
with my pet.

And I win!